"A New Day in the Meadow"

By: Nathan L. Cole

TaTa Books
publishing

The Little Nibbin: A New Day in The Meadow
Copyright © 2014 Nathan L. Cole. All rights reserved.
Published by: TaTa Books
Edited by: Sarah Marie Burnett

ISBN-13: 978-0692341742 (TaTa Books Publishing)
ISBN-10: 0692341749

Printed in the United States of America

www.nlcole.com

It was an ordinary summer day down by the edge of the bright green meadow. The sun was dancing upon the daisies and sparkling across the little puddles that dotted the meadow left from a recent rain shower. The birds were singing and chirping as a breeze blew upon their faces, while the beautiful butterflies danced to and fro, glimmering in the sun.

However, there was something a bit different today. In fact, the day was not ordinary at all, because there was a small, little egg that seemed quite out of place in the meadow. It was just a little bit smaller than a robin's egg, but it was there all the same.

It was so small, in fact, that the other animals didn't even notice that it was there. They were busy doing their daily chores and making plans. The birds were singing and searching for worms. The butterflies were fluttering about. The ants were building their farms. All the while, the egg was still unnoticed by the others.

Then it happened. The little egg began to move slightly, then a bit more, and then a little more, until it was rocking back and forth with a steady motion. All at once it popped open and out hopped a little creature, about the size of a little bug, but this was no bug at all. It seemed as though he was puzzled and was uncertain as to where and who he was.

This little creature had little wings like a bee, but he was no bee. He had big feet that seemed to keep him from flying off, little hands, and the most curious little flower growing from the top of his head.

"Where am I?" the little one thought.

As he began to look around he saw large flowers, plants, and the various animals going to and fro. Still this little one's arrival into the world went unnoticed. He began to notice that each creature was doing something unique.

The birds were singing and sharing their music with the entire meadow. The ants were building their farms and collecting food for the winter. The butterflies were so beautiful as they glimmered in the sun. Everyone had something to do.

So, he wondered, "What is my special thing to do?"

Each one was dedicated to their special purpose.

The little creature said to himself, "I will find my special task as well."

So, off he went, to find his purpose.

9

First, he walked over to the creatures that were working near by. As he got closer, the ants stopped and slowly looked at him with great curiosity.

"Who's you lil fella," asked one of the ant farmers.

"I've come to help," the little one replied.

"So ya thinks ya can work wid us does ya? Well all righty then, get that apple and brings it ova herea."

So, the little guy hopped
over to the great big apple
and with all his might
tried to pick it up. As he tried he umffed, pushed
and even pulled, but with all of his strength he just
could not move the fruit with his little hands, he just
wasn't strong enough. "Perhaps I'm not for collecting,"
he thought.

So, he went off to find something else.

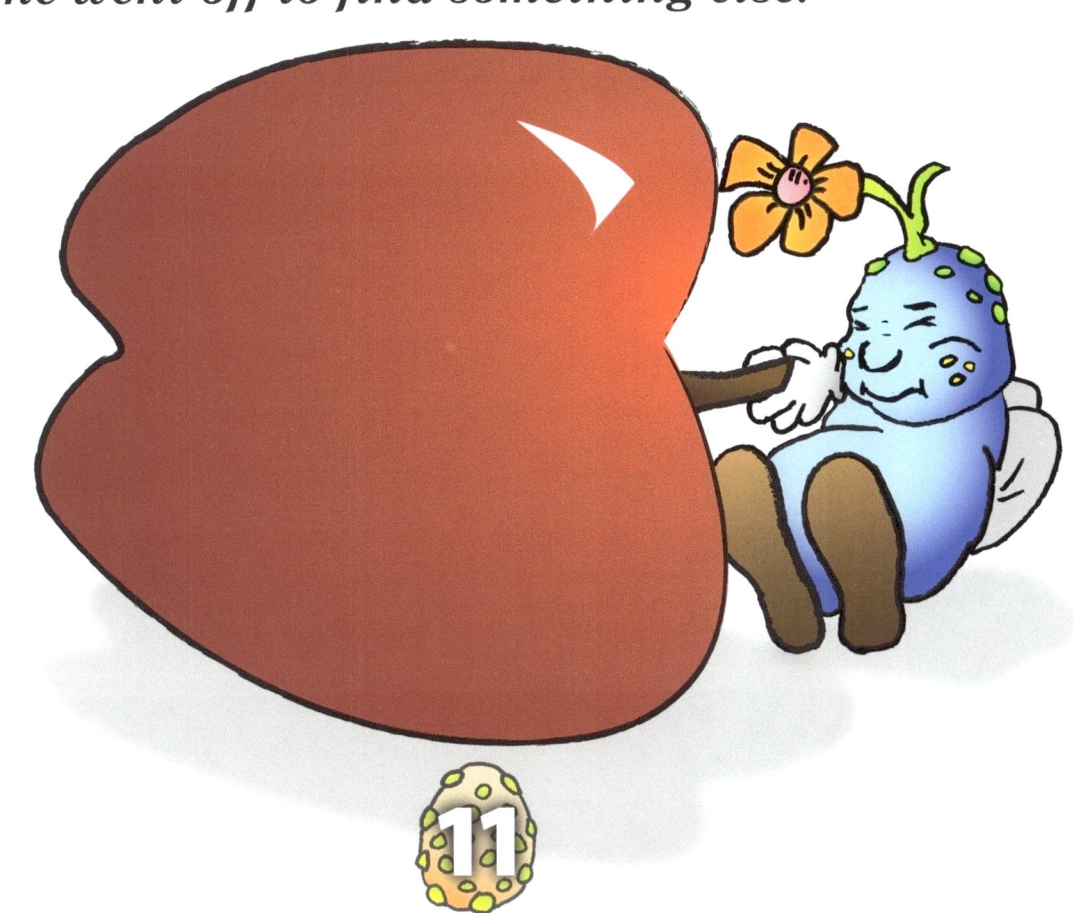

He then saw the beautiful butterflies and how they flew and showed off their beauty in the sun. Though, try as he might he just could not seem to fly as high as they could. His large feet kept pulling him down to the ground.

All he could do was walk, hop, and hover slightly. He then came to the conclusion that his wings were not big and beautiful as the butterflies, nor did they glimmer in the sunshine.

The birds were singing graciously above, so he joined in singing with them, but to the horror all who were around. They ran away covering their ears.

"Maybe my place is not here," he said quietly.

"Of course it's not," said a shriveled voice.

"Who said that," the little one exclaimed.

"I did," said an old grasshopper as he appeared from the shadows of a large sunflower.

"I've been watching you all day.

None of these folk around here can help you. Know why? Because only folk that travel know who you are, and I travel see."

"You know who I am?" the little one asked very politely.

"Sure I do," said the old grasshopper with great certainty. "You're a Nibbin."

"A what?" asked the little creature.

"A Nibbin, they are special creatures that live on the other side of the river past the forest," the grasshopper stated.

"There's a whole valley of ya. I heard about it on my travels, back when I could travel. Now I just sit around here, watching the days go by."

"Well how do I get there?"
the little one asked.

"Don't know fer sure, but there's a path that goes all the way through the Great Woods, and over Quick Creek that they say comes to a valley. In that valley you'll find you're home," he explained.

"Well, thank you. Thank you so very much," said the little one gratefully.

Then, the Little Nibbin set out on his new journey until he came to the farthest edges of the bright green meadow, where he found a path not used by many.

With great hope he thought, "Since there are so many good and wonderful things in this world, someone must have made them, and that maker must have a purpose for me too."

As he continued on the path,
he entered the Great Woods.

22

About The Author

Nathan L. Cole is a devoted husband, father, and the author and illustrator of *The Houlton Saga*, *The Little Nibbin*, and *Jeffry's Story* series—works that explore adventure, courage, hope, and destiny.

Growing up in Iowa, he was inspired early on by classic fantasy and science fiction like *Star Wars* and *The Chronicles of Narnia*.

Holding a degree in theology and with extensive experience in missions, Nathan's writing reflects profound themes and heartfelt depth. Inspired by his bilingual family life and passion for martial arts, he crafts stories that encourage bold imagination, thoughtful reflection, and vision toward worlds yet to come.

"Exploring new worlds, one story at a time!"

www.NLCole.com